Great Clarendon Street, Oxford OX2 6DP

Oxford University Press is a department of the University of Oxford.
It furthers the University's objective of excellence in research, scholarship,
and education by publishing worldwide in

Oxford New York

Auckland Bangkok Buenos Aires Cape Town Chennai Dar es Salaam Delhi Hong Kong Istanbul Karachi Kolkata
Kuala Lumpur Madrid Melbourne Mexico City Mumbai Nairobi São Paulo Shanghai Taipei Tokyo Toronto

Oxford is a registered trade mark of Oxford University Press
in the UK and in certain other countries

First published 2003

British Library Cataloguing in Publication Data available

ISBN 0 19 279124 9 (hardback)
ISBN 0 19 272559 9 (paperback)

2 4 6 8 10 9 7 5 3 1

Typeset in Veljovic.

Colour reproductions by
Dot Gradations Ltd, UK

Printed in Belgium

You can find out more about Jonathan Emmett's
books by visiting his website at
www.scribblestreet.co.uk

To Elizabeth J.E.

To David A.R.

Someone Bigger

Jonathan Emmett

Adrian Reynolds

Sam and Dad had made a kite.
They'd made it large.
They'd made it light.

They went out on a windy day
to see if they could fly it.

'Can I hold it first? Can I?' said Sam.
'I'm old enough – I know I am!'
'No, you're too small!' his dad replied.
'THIS kite needs someone bigger.'

Then Dad let go
and launched the kite,

unwound
the string,
and held it tight,
while Sam stood by,
and watched,
and wished
that he was
someone bigger.

But the wind blew hard.
And the kite flew high.
And pulled Sam's dad **INTO THE SKY.**
And Sam went running after.

'Can I hold it now? Can I?' said Sam.
'I'm old enough – I know I am!'
'No, you're too small!'
his father cried.
'This kite needs
someone bigger.'

The kite flew up above the town,
where people tried to pull it down:

a postman with a sack of mail,
a bank-robber, escaped from jail…

… a policeman riding on a horse,
a bridegroom (and his bride – of course).

But ALL of them were pulled up too!
And Sam went running after.

'Can I hold it now?
Can I?' said Sam.
'I'm old enough –
I know I am!'
'No, you're too small!'
the people cried.
'This kite needs
someone bigger.'

And then, by some strange stroke of luck,
they flew right past a fire truck.

And when the firemen saw the kite,
they grabbed the string and held on tight.

But ALL of them were pulled up too!
And Sam went running after.

'Can I hold it now?
Can I?' said Sam.
'I'm old enough –
I know I am!'
'No, you're too small!'
the firemen cried.
'This kite needs
someone bigger.'

The kite flew on – it would not fall.
It pulled a rhino from its stall …

…and other creatures from the zoo –
a tiger and a kangaroo!

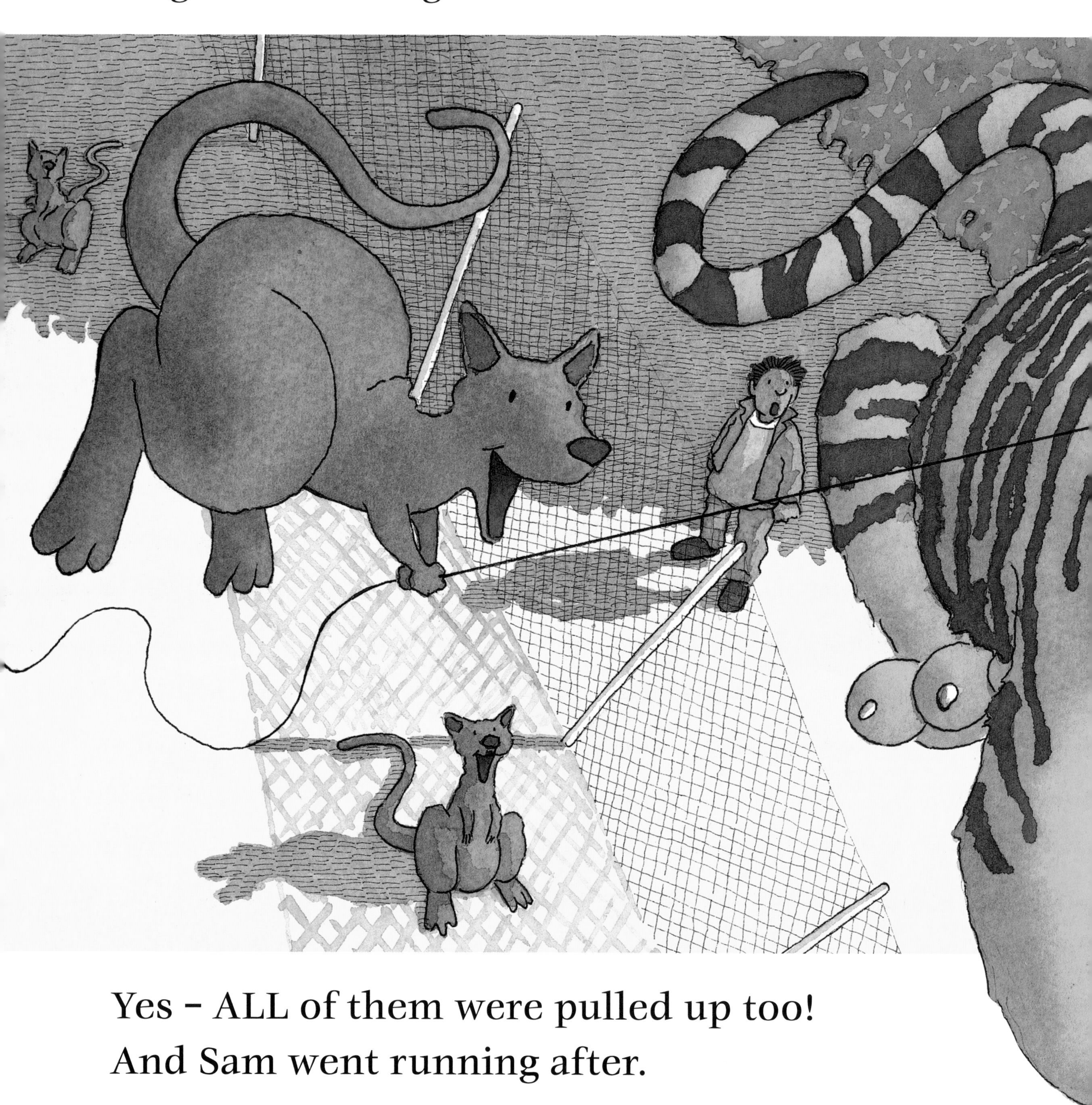

Yes – ALL of them were pulled up too!
And Sam went running after.

'Can I hold it now?
Can I?' said Sam.
'I'm old enough –
I know I am!'
'No, you're too small!'
the creatures cried.
'This kite needs
someone bigger.'

But then Sam caught the kite – at last!
He grabbed the string and held it fast.
And even though he wound and wound,
his feet stayed firmly on the ground!

And, one by one, they came back down,
everyone from zoo and town:

rhino, tiger, kangaroo,
firemen, bride (and bridegroom too),

postman, robber, policeman, horse,

and last of all, Sam's dad – of course!

'I'll hold it now,' said Sam, 'because
I'm old enough – I knew I was!
I'm not too small, and as you see,
this kite needs someone

JUST

LIKE

ME!'